Stories for Seniors

STORIES FOR SENIORS

First edition. March 15, 2023.

Copyright © 2023 Liom Liom.

ISBN: 979-8215546871

Written by Liom Liom.

The wonders of age

Once upon a time, there was a group of senior citizens living in a retirement home. Many of them felt lonely and unhappy, and wished they could be young again. But one day they discovered that old age also has its wonders.

It all started when one of the residents, Mr. Müller, resumed his old hobbies. He began to write poetry and take an interest in painting. The other residents were amazed at how lively he suddenly seemed and decided to do the same. Soon after, they too discovered their passions and began to get involved in various activities. Ms. Schneider started doing yoga, Mr. Schmidt began playing the guitar, and Ms. Fischer started sewing her own clothes.

Seniors learned that age need not be a barrier to new experiences and adventures. On the contrary, it can be a time of discovery and growth. They began to improve their skills and engage in new challenges.

One day they decided to show off their new talents and hold an exhibition at the retirement home. It was a great success and they received many compliments from the other residents and also from their families. The seniors were proud of their achievements and felt more alive and happy than ever before.

The wonders of old age were far from over. The seniors formed a choir and began to take trips into nature. They realized that life still had so much to offer and that they should not stop looking for new experiences.

The seniors in the retirement home learned that old age does not mean the end. It can be a time of discovery and growth if you let it. They found joy and happiness in their passions and abilities, proving that you're never too old to learn something new.

The walk in the park

Mrs. Berger was a fun-loving retiree who used every day to stay active and enjoy life to the fullest. One sunny day, she decided to take a walk in the park and enjoy nature.

When she arrived at the park, she was able to enjoy the fresh air and the scent of the flowers as she leisurely strolled through the paths. She watched birds singing in the trees and children playing in the playground.

During her walk, Mrs. Berger noticed that an elderly man sitting on a park bench looked very sad. She decided to keep him company and sat down next to him. She introduced herself and started a conversation with him. He told her about his wife, who had recently passed away, and that he felt lonely.

Mrs. Berger realized that the man needed someone to talk to and offered him her company. Together they strolled through the park, chatting and laughing. They visited the pond and fed the ducks before sitting down on a bench to enjoy the sun.

When they said goodbye, the man thanked her warmly for her company and said that he felt much better. Mrs. Berger was happy that she could help someone and returned home with a big smile on her face.

In the weeks that followed, Mrs. Berger visited the park regularly and met with the man again and again. Over time, they became friends and helped each other overcome loneliness. They shared their experiences and stories and enjoyed each other's company.

That walk in the park had changed the lives of Mrs. Berger and the older man in ways they had never expected. They were both happy and grateful for the new friendship they had found.

The small gazebo

Mr. Schmidt had always been an avid gardener. Since his retirement, he had more time to take care of his garden, which he lovingly tended. One day, he discovered a small, old gazebo in the garden that was in a haunted state. Mr. Schmidt decided to restore it and make it a cozy place to relax and enjoy the garden.

He began to tear down the old boards and repair the floor. He bought new material and spent many hours renovating the gazebo. Finally, it was back in full glory and Mr. Schmidt was thrilled with his work.

One day, Mr. Schmidt decided to invite his friends and neighbors to a picnic in the gazebo. He prepared sandwiches, cakes and tea and decorated the gazebo with flowers and candles. When his guests arrived, they marveled at the transformation of the small gazebo and were impressed by Mr. Schmidt's work.

They enjoyed the picnic, the beautiful weather and the charm of the garden. Mr. Schmidt proudly showed them the plants and flowers he had planted and told them stories from his long gardening career.

During the picnic, Mr. Schmidt noticed that he had lost one of his gardening gloves. They searched the garden together and finally found the glove in a rose bed. When they picked up the glove, they found a small box buried underneath.

When they opened the box, they found an old handwritten note that came from a previous resident of the house. The note said that the gazebo had once been the family's favorite place to gather and make memories.

Mr. Schmidt and his guests were touched by the story and decided to continue the tradition and make the gazebo a place where family and friends could meet. From that day on, the little gazebo became a popular place for gatherings, birthday parties and garden parties.

For Mr. Schmidt, restoring the gazebo was not just physical labor, but an opportunity to create memories and foster friendships. The little gazebo brought joy and happiness into his life and that of his friends and neighbors, and became a place of love and community.

A night in nature

Mr. Müller and his wife had always been avid nature lovers. They had often gone on hikes and enjoyed the beauty of nature. But over the years it had become more difficult to go on longer hikes and they missed the feeling of being out in nature.

One day they decided to go on a camping trip and spend a night in nature. They packed their tent, sleeping bags and camping equipment and drove to a nearby nature park.

When they arrived, they were overwhelmed by the beauty of the park. They hiked through the forest, along mountain trails and past clear lakes. They saw deer and other animals and enjoyed the silence and tranquility of nature.

When it was time to pitch the tent, they chose an idyllic spot on the edge of the lake. They set up their tent and prepared a campfire. They cooked soup and roasted sausages on the open fire and enjoyed eating outdoors.

While sitting by the fire, they noticed that the sky was full of stars and they could enjoy the feeling of freedom and peace. Mr. Müller told his wife about his memories of his childhood and his summer vacations when he camped in the mountains with his parents and siblings.

They spent the night in the tent, listening to the sound of the wind and the lapping of the lake, enjoying the feeling of freedom and independence. In the morning they woke up when the sun rose and they decided to spend another day in the park.

They continued to wander, discovering new places and enjoying nature. They felt more alive and free than they had in a long time. When it was time to return, they were filled with a sense of joy and gratitude for the beauty and freedom that nature had given them.

For Mr. Müller and his wife, this night in nature was an unforgettable experience. It reminded them of their youth and the feeling of being alive and free. It also gave them the feeling that it is never too late to dare something new and to cultivate their love for nature.

The change of weather

Mrs. Schröder had been a big fan of the weather for many years. She watched the sky every day to see what clouds were moving there and what kind of weather they heralded. But lately, she felt like the weather was changing. It didn't seem to be as predictable as it used to be.

One day she decided to write down her observations. She made a list of the different types of clouds and weather situations and began to write them down each day. As she did so, she noticed that the weather was indeed different than before. There were more unexpected thunderstorms, storms, and unusually warm days.

But instead of getting angry, she decided to make the best of the situation. She began to see the weather as an opportunity to discover new things. On days when it rained, she read a good book or spent time with her family. On sunny days, she went for a walk in the park or visited her friends.

She also became interested in weather and researched what changes in the world might affect the weather. She read about climate change and how we can all help protect the weather and the environment.

One day, Mrs. Schröder had an idea. She decided to start a weather group for seniors to share her knowledge and experience with others. She invited friends and neighbors and they met every month to discuss the weather and climate change. They also invited experts to talk about different topics.

Over time, Mrs. Schröder noticed that she had changed not only the weather, but also her relationships with other people and her community. She was happier and felt more fulfilled than ever before. She had found a new passion and was able to help others get excited about it, too.

The change in weather had led Ms. Schröder to discover new ways to use her time and enrich her life. She had accepted the challenges and grown from them. And the best part was that she was able to share this with others, improving everyone's lives.

An encounter in the city

Mrs. Müller had become accustomed to being alone in recent years. She was an elderly woman who lived in the city and often did her shopping alone. One day she was on her way to the supermarket when she was approached by a young woman.

"Excuse me, can you tell me where the nearest pharmacy is?" the woman asked politely.

Mrs. Müller was surprised to be approached by someone and kindly replied, "Yes, the pharmacy is just a few streets away. If you like, I can show you the way."

The young woman was relieved and grateful for the offer. Together they walked through the streets of the city and talked about God and the world. They found that they had a lot in common and enjoyed each other's company.

When they finally reached the pharmacy, the young woman thanked Mrs. Müller warmly for her help and for the nice conversation. Mrs. Müller was happy to have met someone who drove away her loneliness for a short time.

Over the next few weeks, Mrs. Müller and the young woman met again and again in the city. They went shopping together, visited museums together and went to the movies. Mrs. Müller felt that she had made a new friend and was grateful for the unexpected encounter in the city.

Over time, Ms. Müller learned that it is never too late to make new friends. She had learned that you have to be open to meeting new people. And that there were still surprises and opportunities in the city where she had lived for so long.

The encounter in the city had shown Ms. Müller that life is full of surprises and adventures if you only let it be. And she had found a new friend who had enriched her life.

The beauty of nature

Mr. Schmidt always had a love for nature. He loved being outside and admiring the beauty of nature. One day he decided to go on a hike in the mountains to experience nature up close.

He packed his backpack with everything he needed for the hike and set off. The climb was strenuous, but Mr. Schmidt was determined to reach his destination. He hiked through dense forests and across crystal clear streams, enjoying the breathtaking views of the mountains.

When he finally reached the top, he was speechless. The view was breathtaking and he couldn't help but feel a deep sense of gratitude. He felt happy and fulfilled, and he knew that he would never forget this moment.

As he sat on the summit, he enjoyed the beauty of nature and let the peace and quiet take over. He felt his mind become calmer and more relaxed, and he felt more alive than he had in a long time.

When he finally returned to the valley on foot, he felt changed. He had found a deeper connection to nature and to himself. He felt that he had experienced something special and that he could be grateful for having had the opportunity to experience the beauty of nature in such an immediate and intense way.

Mr. Schmidt knew that he wanted to have many more adventures in nature, and he was sure that he would never stop admiring and appreciating the beauty of nature. He had found a deep appreciation for life and what it had to offer. And he knew that through the beauty of nature he would experience many more happy and fulfilling moments.

A day at the zoo

Mrs. Meier has always had a passion for animals. When she heard that the local zoo was being expanded, she couldn't wait to visit.

On a sunny day, Ms. Meier set out for the zoo. She had a camera and a notebook with her to record her observations. As she stepped through the front gate, she was overwhelmed by the variety of animals and the beauty of the grounds.

She started her tour at the aquarium and was fascinated by the colorful fish and the majestic sharks. Then she went to the monkeys and watched them play and groom each other. Ms. Meier couldn't help but smile and feel the joy of the animals.

Next, she visited the lions and the elephants, which were so majestic and sublime. She was impressed by their power and beauty. Ms. Meier took many photos and wrote down her observations in her notebook.

As she continued to wander through the zoo, she discovered many other animals and watched how they moved and interacted. She could feel the happiness and joy that these animals radiated, and she felt so happy and fulfilled herself.

When the day ended and the zoo closed, Mrs. Meier was happy and satisfied. She had spent a wonderful day at the zoo and couldn't wait to return and discover more. She knew that by visiting the zoo and observing the animals, she had found a deeper appreciation for nature and for life itself.

The journey into the unknown

Mrs. Schneider was a spry retiree who had always stuck to plans and routines in her life. One day, however, she decided it was time to bring some adventure into her life. She packed her bag and set off on a journey into the unknown.

At first, Ms. Schneider was unsure where the trip should go. She bought a map and let her heart decide. In the end, she decided on a city by the sea that she had never visited before.

The trip was not easy for Ms. Schneider. She had to travel by public transport, stay in a strange hotel and find her way around an unfamiliar city. But she was determined not to let it get her down.

When she finally arrived in the city, she quickly took a liking to her destination. She walked along the beach, explored the alleys and sampled local specialties. She met other travelers and locals and had many interesting conversations.

One day she met an elderly gentleman named Herr Schmidt. He told her about a secret garden on the outskirts of town that only a few people knew about. Ms. Schneider became curious and decided to visit the garden.

When she reached the garden, she was overwhelmed by its beauty. There were colorful flowers, exotic plants and a pond with golden fish. She felt happy and free and knew that this journey into the unknown had been the best decision of her life.

When Ms. Schneider returned, she told her friends and family about her journey. She told them that she had learned that it was important in life to break out of the comfort zone sometimes and to dare the unknown. She decided that in the future she would travel more often to see new places and meet new people. She was happy and fulfilled and knew that this trip had changed her life.

Life in the country

Mrs. Meier was an elderly lady who had spent her whole life in the city. One day she decided to escape the hustle and bustle of the city and move to the countryside. She had always dreamed of living in a small cottage with a garden where she could take care of animals and plants.

When she found the little house, it was love at first sight. It was exactly what she had been looking for. She moved in and began to enjoy her life in the country.

Working on the land was hard, but Mrs. Meier found joy in every task. She took care of her chickens, pigs and cows and planted fruits and vegetables in her garden. She learned how to make jam and how to make sausage. She finally had time to do things that were really important to her.

Ms. Meier also made new friends in the countryside. She met her neighbors, who helped her find her way around the area and showed her how to prepare traditional dishes. She attended the local church and became part of the community.

One day she decided to have a small party to thank her new friends. She invited all her neighbors and friends and prepared a feast. There was sausage, potatoes, bread and homemade jam. Everyone was delighted with the food and the ambience that Mrs. Meier had created.

When the party was over, Mrs. Meier felt happier and more fulfilled than ever before. She had finally found the life she had always dreamed of. She enjoyed every day in the country and was grateful for all the new friends and experiences she had made.

The visit of the grandson

Mrs. Müller was sitting in her armchair and looking out the window. It was a sunny day and she watched the birds hopping around on the trees in front of her house. But despite the beautiful weather, she felt lonely and missed her family.

Suddenly, the doorbell rang. Mrs. Müller rose slowly and opened the door. Standing in front of her was her grandson Felix, who had paid her a surprise visit. Mrs. Müller was overjoyed and embraced him warmly.

Felix hadn't stopped by his grandma's house in a long time. He told her about his experiences and showed her photos from his last vacation. Mrs. Müller listened attentively and laughed at the funny stories.

Together they went into the garden and spent the day drinking tea, eating cake and talking about old times. Mrs. Müller told about her own experiences as a young woman and Felix listened spellbound.

When it started to get dark, Felix brought his grandma back into the house and helped her with dinner. They continued talking and laughing together about the latest jokes.

When it was time for Felix to leave, he hugged his grandma once more and promised to come by again soon. Mrs. Müller was overjoyed and finally felt really alive again.

Over the next few weeks, they called each other often and told each other about their experiences. Mrs. Müller no longer felt so lonely and looked forward to her grandson's next visit every time.

Visiting her grandmother became a weekly routine for Felix and a moment of happiness for Mrs. Müller that enriched her life. They enjoyed the time they spent together and made plans for further experiences together.

This was the beginning of a new and wonderful relationship between grandma and grandson. A relationship that held endless joy, happiness and excitement for both.

The love in old age

Mrs. Berger lived alone in her house on the outskirts of town. She had been widowed for a long time and had no one at her side since the death of her husband. Although she was a strong and independent woman, she often felt lonely and missed the closeness of a partner.

One day, Mrs. Berger met Mr. Schmitt, a widower from her neighborhood, in the supermarket. They knew each other fleetingly by sight, but had never really spoken to each other. But somehow they fell into conversation and it turned out that they had many interests in common.

In the following weeks, they met more often by chance in the supermarket or while walking in the park. They began to get to know each other better and quickly found that they got along well.

One day, Mr. Schmitt invited Mrs. Berger for coffee. She was nervous and excited, but also curious about what was to come. Over coffee and cake, they spent hours talking and getting to know each other better.

When the evening came, they said goodbye and Mrs. Berger felt that something special had developed between them. In the weeks that followed, they met regularly and learned more and more about each other.

They went for walks together, visited museums and concerts, and even spent Christmas together. Their love for each other grew steadily and they finally felt complete again.

There were moments of uncertainty and doubt, but they knew they needed each other and that their love was strong enough to overcome any challenges.

And so they spent happy years together, discovering the world together and enjoying the beautiful sides of life. They supported each other in difficult moments and knew that they would always stand by each other.

At the age of over 80, they celebrated their wedding to seal their love for each other. They were the perfect example that it is never too late to find the love of your life. For Mrs. Berger and Mr. Schmitt, it was a happy ending to a wonderful love story that began in old age.

The journey into the past

Mrs. Schmidt was already over 80 years old and had lived a full life. But there was one thing that preoccupied her all her life: her childhood sweetheart Thomas. They had met in the 1950s, when they were both still young and carefree. They spent an unforgettable time together, but in the end they parted ways when Thomas took a job overseas.

Mrs. Schmidt had never heard from him since, but she could never forget him. She often thought of him and wondered how he had fared and whether he was still alive.

One day, while looking through old mementos in the attic, she came across an old letter from Thomas. It had never arrived because she had already moved by then. The letter contained an invitation to visit him overseas.

Mrs. Schmidt was excited and decided to accept the invitation. With the help of her granddaughter, she organized the trip and set off.

When she arrived, Thomas was overwhelmed by her arrival. They spent an unforgettable week together, catching up on the past years and sharing about their lives.

It was a trip down memory lane, but it felt like time had stopped. Mrs. Schmidt and Thomas discovered that they still felt a lot for each other and decided that they would keep in touch.

Back in her hometown, Ms. Schmidt felt like a different person. She had finally come to terms with her past and knew that she no longer had to worry about Thomas. She had finally found peace with her past.

And so she spent her last years happy and content, knowing that she had finally found her childhood sweetheart again and that he was still an important part of her life. It was a journey into the past that changed her life and gave her a new sense of freedom and happiness.

A day at the beach

It was a sunny day in late summer when Mrs. Meier decided to go to the beach. She had always enjoyed being by the sea, but lately she had the feeling that she too rarely took time for such things.

When she arrived at the beach, she spread out her blanket and sat down in the sand. She looked at the calm sea and took a deep breath. It was a quiet and peaceful moment in which she could forget all her worries and fears.

But suddenly she heard a familiar voice behind her. It was her former school friend, Mr. Müller, whom she had not seen for years. They had been inseparable in school, but had gone their separate ways after graduation.

They talked for hours and told each other about their lives in recent years. Mr. Müller told her about his wife and grandchildren, while Mrs. Meier told of her travels and adventures.

It was a beautiful day at the beach, where they felt like two teenagers who had just started life. They laughed and enjoyed the wonderful weather, the rushing sea and the carefree atmosphere.

When the day came to an end, they said goodbye and promised to stay in touch. Mrs. Meier was happy that she had met Mr. Müller and that she could once again remember old times.

She returned home knowing that it's never too late to rekindle old friendships and that there are still so many adventures to be had, if you're willing to go for it.

And so she decided to go to the beach more often and enjoy life, even in old age.

The adventures of everyday life

Mr. Müller had always been an adventurer, but since he had retired, he felt that he was missing the adventures of everyday life. He had traveled a lot and visited many countries, but now he longed for something new, something exciting and yet familiar.

One day he decided to look at everyday life as an adventure and focus on the little things in life. He started exploring new places in his city, visiting new restaurants and discovering new hobbies.

For example, he went to the local park and watched the birds and squirrels, he visited the museum and read books about history and culture. He also started doing yoga regularly and inviting friends over for coffee to talk and laugh together.

One day, while walking in the park, he met a young woman named Sophie. She was an artist and had an exhibition in town. They talked for hours about art, music and life in general.

Sophie showed him her artwork and Mr. Müller was amazed by her creativity and talent. She invited him to work with her on a project and so they began to create works of art together.

The adventures of everyday life had brought Mr. Müller back to his passion for life and his curiosity about what he would encounter. He no longer had the feeling that he was retired, but that he had started a new chapter in his life, full of discoveries and joy.

And so he learned that adventures don't always have to be great journeys or spectacular events, but that life itself is full of adventures if you are willing to discover and enjoy them.

The power of music

Mrs. Schneider had loved music all her life. She played the piano and sang in a choir, but in old age she had difficulty practicing her passion due to health problems.

One day she heard a young musician playing on the street. His voice and guitar playing were so impressive that Ms. Schneider couldn't help but listen. The musician, Max, had an incredible energy and passion for music that immediately reminded Ms. Schneider of her own love for music.

She asked him if he could give her lessons, and he agreed. Max showed her new techniques and songs she had never heard before. With his help, Ms. Schneider learned to improve her skills on the piano and to sing new songs.

They met regularly and played together. The music made them laugh, cry and dance. Mrs. Schneider felt young again and full of energy when she felt the sounds of the music.

As she shared her new passion with friends and family, they realized how happy and alive she had become again. Music had an incredible power to change her life and bring her joy.

Max and Mrs. Schneider performed together in a local concert and delighted the audience with their passion and music. It was an unforgettable moment for Mrs. Schneider, and she was grateful that through the power of music she had found a new passion that had enriched her life.

The trip to the city

Mrs. Berger had not felt that she had been properly in the city for years. She had always lived in a small village and rarely had the chance to visit the big city. But on this day, the time had finally come. Together with her friends, she had planned a trip to the city.

Mrs. Berger was excited, but also a little scared. The city was so big and busy, and she was afraid she might get lost. But her friends were always by her side and helped her find her way.

They visited museums, parks and restaurants and enjoyed the hustle and bustle of the city. Ms. Berger was thrilled by the diversity and energy of the city. Everywhere there was something to discover and experience.

As they strolled through the streets, they suddenly heard the sounds of music. A group of young musicians were playing in the street and attracting a crowd. Mrs. Berger and her friends joined them and began to dance. It was an indescribable feeling to dance and laugh with complete strangers.

When the day came to an end, everyone was exhausted, but also happy and filled with the new experiences. Mrs. Berger felt that she had finally taken part in life again and felt young and full of energy again.

From that day on, they visited regularly and enjoyed every minute. It was a wonderful adventure that they would not forget.

The discovery of the unknown

Mr. Müller has always had a penchant for adventure. When he found a mysterious map that led to a hidden treasure, he could hardly believe his luck. He had dreamed of going on a treasure hunt since he was a child, but never thought he would get this chance.

Together with his friends, he set out to find the treasure. They crossed forests, hiked over mountains and followed the river to a hidden valley. The way was arduous and exhausting, but they were determined to find the treasure.

When they finally reached the valley, they saw a ruined tower standing on a hill. Mr. Müller sensed that they would find the treasure there. They climbed the steep steps and discovered a secret chamber inside the tower.

There they found a box full of gold coins and precious stones. Mr. Müller could hardly believe his luck. His friends' joy was as great as his own.

But it was not only the treasure that made her happy. It was the discovery of the unknown that invigorated them and awakened their spirit of adventure. They felt that life still had so much to offer and that they could still make many discoveries.

The way back was easier and they enjoyed every moment of the adventure. Mr. Müller and his friends were happy and grateful that they could share this experience together. They decided to have many more adventures and knew that life still had many surprises in store for them.

The beauty of art

Ms. Schneider had always been passionate about art. Every time she was in a gallery or museum, she felt like she was in another world. She loved admiring the beauty of the works of art and being inspired by them.

One day she heard about an exhibition that was taking place in the city. It was a retrospective of the famous artist Max Klinger. Mrs. Schneider could hardly believe her luck. Max Klinger was one of her favorite artists, and she had always dreamed of seeing his works in an exhibition one day.

She invited her friends to go to the exhibition with her. They all had a common interest in art and were eager to see the works of Max Klinger.

When they arrived at the exhibition, they were overwhelmed by the beauty of the artworks. The colors, the shapes, and the textures of the paintings and sculptures fascinated them. They were so engrossed in the art that they forgot about time and spent hours in the exhibition.

When they finally went outside, they felt fulfilled and happy. They had found a new appreciation for the beauty of art and its ability to evoke emotion. They realized that art was not just a decoration for the walls, but a way to enrich life and understand the world around us.

Ms. Schneider and her friends were grateful for the experience. They decided to visit art exhibitions together more often and share their passion for art. They knew that the beauty of art would bring them many more happy moments.

The visit to the doctor

Mrs. Meier had not been to the doctor for years. She felt healthy and vital and had no complaints. But her son had advised her to have regular checkups. "You never know what's going on in your body," he had said.

Mrs. Meier decided to take his advice and made an appointment with the doctor. She was nervous because she had never had a checkup before. She was afraid that the doctor might find something she didn't expect.

When she arrived at the doctor's office, she was greeted by a friendly physician's assistant. She felt a little reassured and relaxed when she was called into the doctor's office.

The doctor, Dr. Müller, introduced himself and asked Ms. Meier how she was feeling. He examined her thoroughly and did some tests. Ms. Meier felt well taken care of and in good hands.

After the examination, Dr. Müller told her: "Mrs. Meier, I am pleased to inform you that you are in the best of health. There are no signs of illness or any problems. You can rest easy."

Mrs. Meier could hardly believe her luck. She was so relieved and grateful. She had been so worried and was now relieved to learn that everything was okay.

She thanked Dr. Müller and left the practice with a smile on her face. She knew that in the future she would go to the doctor regularly to maintain her health. She had learned that it was important to take care of herself and look after her body. She was grateful for this visit to the doctor and the feeling that everything was okay.

The challenges of life

In a small town there lived a group of senior citizens who met regularly at the local community center to spend their free time together. It was a cheerful group that supported each other and was there for each other.

One day they decided to go hiking together in the nearby mountains. Most of them had not hiked for a long time, but they were ready for a new challenge. The anticipation was great and they prepared well.

The hike was exhausting, but they were delighted by the beautiful nature and breathtaking views. They helped each other and always encouraged each other to go on.

When they reached the top, they sat down exhausted on a rock and enjoyed the view of the landscape. It was a special moment that connected them all.

Suddenly it started to rain and they had to hurry to go back down the mountain. It was more difficult than they thought, because the path was slippery and dangerous. But they made it together and were proud of their achievement.

Back at the community center, they sat together contentedly and shared their experiences. They agreed that life holds challenges, but it is worth accepting them and mastering them together.

They decided to set out on many more adventures and to tackle life's challenges together. Because they knew: together they could do anything.

The dream of flying

Mr. Müller sat on his porch and watched the sky. He remembered the dream he had as a young man, of flying. But with age, that dream seemed out of reach. His eyes were not as sharp, his bones not as flexible, and his heart not as strong as it was then. But still, he couldn't stop dreaming about it.

One day, Mr. Müller decided to get a little closer to his dream and signed up for a paragliding course. Although he felt insecure at first, he was thrilled by the fascination of flying. With each flight, he became more courageous and self-confident.

One day, during a flight, Mr. Müller noticed that he was no longer flying alone. A young hawk flew beside him and accompanied him on his journey. Mr. Müller could hardly believe his luck and joy. The hawk stayed with him until he landed safely.

Since that day, Mr. Müller flew regularly and each time the falcon accompanied him on his journey. Mr. Müller felt as free as a bird and was grateful for the fulfillment of his dream.

One day he invited his grandchildren and showed them how he could glide through the air. The grandchildren looked at their grandfather with admiration and were impressed by his strength and determination.

Mr. Müller had learned that it is never too late to realize one's dreams. Even at an advanced age, there is still so much to discover and experience. Life is a journey that never ends and Mr.

Müller had learned to see every challenge as an opportunity and to always keep going, no matter how old you are.

The journey to the distance

Marianne always had the dream of traveling the world. When she was young, however, she couldn't afford it, and later, as a single pensioner, she had no one who wanted to travel with her. But now she had decided to realize her dream before it was too late.

So Marianne set out for her local travel agency and booked a trip to faraway places. She had decided on a cruise through the Pacific, during which she would visit numerous exotic places.

When the day of departure arrived, Marianne felt excited and a little nervous. But when she boarded the ship and met the friendly crew and other passengers, she immediately felt at ease.

Days passed and Marianne visited incredible places she had never heard of before. She saw crystal clear waters, white sand beaches and colorful coral reefs. She made new friends and enjoyed life aboard the ship.

But there were also challenges, such as when she got lost on a hike and ended up having to be brought back to the ship by the rescue service. But even in difficult situations, Marianne always found the strength to be happy and stay positive.

Finally, Marianne returned from her journey far away, rich in new experiences and memories. She had learned that life is full of surprises and challenges, but also full of joy and beauty if you let yourself go with it and experience it with an open heart and curiosity. And who knows, maybe soon she would be planning her next trip again.

The memories of times gone by

It was a sunny afternoon in autumn when Mr. Schmidt was sitting in his favorite armchair and leafing through old photo albums. He was reminiscing about times gone by and all the wonderful experiences he had had in his life. But then a photo caught his eye that touched him in a very special way. It showed him as a young man together with his wife, who had unfortunately passed away a few years ago. They were standing in front of a large castle in France, where they had spent their honeymoon.

Mr. Schmidt spontaneously decided to travel there once again and remember the time he spent together with his wife. He planned everything down to the smallest detail and finally took the train to France. When he arrived at the castle, he immediately felt a deep connection to the place and told the other visitors about his memories.

But then something incredible happened. As he walked through the corridors of the castle, he suddenly heard a voice that seemed very familiar. He followed it and finally found himself in front of an old door. When he opened it, he saw his wife sitting in a room surrounded by all her favorite things.

She told him that she was not really dead, but living in a kind of parallel world. She had been waiting for him to travel through time together once again and relive all the memories. Mr. Schmidt could hardly believe it, but he knew that this was a chance he could not miss.

So they spent some wonderful days together and visited all the places where they had once spent their honeymoon. They laughed, cried and told each other stories from their shared past. It was a time full of joy and happiness, and Mr. Schmidt was infinitely grateful for this gift.

In the end, he had to say goodbye to his wife and return to reality. But he knew that he would never forget her and that she would always remain in his heart. He returned home with a wealth of memories and a deep sense of gratitude for all the wonderful years he had spent with his wife.

The visit to the museum

Mrs. Schröder had long wanted to visit her city's museum. Even as a child, she had dreamed of doing so, but in her youth she had never had the opportunity. Now, at retirement age, she wanted to finally fulfill this dream.

When she arrived at the museum, she immediately felt like she was in another world. The paintings and sculptures impressed her deeply. They reminded her of her childhood, when she herself had loved to paint.

Mrs. Schröder wandered from room to room, looking at each work of art with great admiration. In the process, she met an older gentleman who was also visiting the museum alone. They struck up a conversation and quickly realized that they shared a passion for art. The gentleman explained to her the background of some of the works and they shared their impressions.

After visiting all the exhibition rooms, Mrs. Schröder and the gentleman sat down in the museum café. There they told each other about their life stories and laughed about past experiences. Mrs. Schröder felt her loneliness slowly dissolve and she established a new connection with another person.

When they finally said goodbye to each other, Mrs. Schröder knew that she had not only visited the museum, but had also met a wonderful person. The day had brought her not only new insights into art and history, but also joy and happiness through an unexpected encounter.

Everyday life in the nursing home

The sun shines brightly through the nursing home's window, casting a warm glow over the room. Mrs. Müller, a resident of the home, sits in a corner and looks sadly out of the window. She thinks back to the days when she was independent and could do anything she wanted. Now she feels lonely and confined.

Suddenly, a group of volunteers enters the home and starts talking to the residents and offering activities. Mrs. Müller is skeptical, but her interest is piqued when she hears that they can participate in a music workshop.

The volunteers bring instruments and start playing music. Mrs. Müller listens and is carried away by the sounds. She feels her spirits lift and her heart is filled with joy.

When the workshop comes to an end, Ms. Müller is surprised at how quickly the time has passed. She is grateful for the experience and feels inspired. The volunteers promise to come back soon, and Mrs. Müller is looking forward to more adventures at the nursing home.

She realizes that joy and happiness can also be found in everyday life in a nursing home if one is open to new experiences and focuses on the positive. Music has shown her that life can still be full of surprises and joy, even in old age.

The experiences in the garden

It was a sunny day in spring and the residents of the nursing home had decided to spend the day in the garden. They sat on comfortable chairs under shady trees and enjoyed the warm sunshine. Some of them were reading a book, others were chatting with each other and still others were watching the birds flying through the garden.

When suddenly one of the residents, Mrs. Meier, stood up and said, "You know what? I want to make a bed and grow vegetables!" The others looked at her in surprise, but soon they all agreed enthusiastically.

They immediately began preparations and soon the bed was ready for planting. Each resident chose a vegetable he or she wanted to plant, and then the work began. There was digging, weeding and watering, and everyone helped in his or her own way.

The days passed and the bed began to grow. The residents watched with joy as their vegetables grew bigger and bigger. And when harvest time came, everyone was excited. They picked the tomatoes, cucumbers, zucchini and carrots and had their hands full.

In the evening, everyone gathered in the dining room and enjoyed a delicious vegetable dish from their own harvest. It was a wonderful feeling to have created and harvested something and they were all proud of themselves.

This experience in the garden had shown them that even in old age new adventures and challenges await them. It was a valuable experience that gave them joy and happiness and showed them that life in a retirement home also has its beautiful sides.

The day with the grandchildren

In a small village lived an old woman named Hilde. She was already in her seventies and had lived a full life. But there was something she was missing - grandchildren. Hilde had no children of her own, and her relatives lived far away and had no children of their own. But Hilde did not give up hope of having grandchildren one day.

One day Hilde received a call from an old acquaintance whom she had not seen for many years. The acquaintance had two grandchildren who lived near Hilde and would like to visit their great-aunt. Hilde was incredibly happy and immediately planned a special day with the grandchildren.

On the day of the visit Hilde was excited like a little child. She prepared a picnic and bought sweets and small gifts for the children. When the grandchildren finally arrived, Hilde was overjoyed. The children were delighted with their great aunt and enjoyed the picnic together in the garden.

Afterwards, they went on a short hike in the nearby forest. Hilde told the children stories from her childhood and the children hung on her every word. Hilde enjoyed the time with the grandchildren and completely forgot how old she actually was. The children played, ran around and had a lot of fun.

When the day ended, everyone was tired but happy. Hilde told the children that they could come back anytime and that she was already looking forward to the next meeting. The grandchildren said their fond farewells and Hilde watched them go until they disappeared from sight.

Hilde was so grateful for this special day with the grandchildren. She felt that her life had meaning again and that she could still experience much joy and happiness, even though she was older. Hilde knew that she would never forget this day and that it would bring her joy and happiness for a long time to come.

The meeting with new people

Anna had been widowed for many years and lived alone in her apartment. She had long wanted to meet new people and surround herself with them. But she didn't quite know how to go about it.

One day, Anna decided to summon up her courage and set off for the city. There she spotted an ad for an event for seniors where you could meet new people. Anna was hesitant at first, but then she overcame her fear and decided to attend the event.

When she got there, she was greeted by a nice lady who welcomed her warmly. Anna was relieved and started talking to the other participants. She met so many different people who all had an interesting story to tell.

An elderly gentleman named Max caught her eye in particular. Max had been a pensioner for many years and had experienced a lot. Anna and Max got to talking and it turned out that they had common interests. They talked for hours and Anna had the feeling that she had found a new friend.

At the end of the event, Anna and Max exchanged phone numbers and arranged to go for a walk together the next week. Anna was overjoyed and felt that her life was finally moving in a positive direction again.

The week passed quickly and soon it was time for the meeting with Max. Anna was excited and made her way to the agreed meeting place. When she saw Max, he waved happily at her and they both knew it was going to be a special day.

They walked through the park together, enjoying nature and talking about God and the world. Anna had the feeling that she hadn't been this happy in years. Max was a true treasure and she felt that she had known him for years.

At the end of the day, they said goodbye warmly and Anna knew that they would meet again soon. She was grateful for meeting Max and knew that she would meet many more exciting people. Anna was happy and ready to embrace life and all its possibilities.

The joy of nature

Hans had been an avid nature lover for many years. He loved to walk through forests, observe animals and enjoy the beauty of nature. When he retired, he finally had more time to pursue his hobbies.

One day Hans decided to take a trip to the mountains. He packed his hiking boots, his camera and enough provisions and set off. The sun was shining, the sky was blue, and Hans felt his spirits rising by the minute.

When he reached the mountains, he was overwhelmed by the beauty of the landscape. He walked through forests, across meadows and along streams. The air was fresh and clear and Hans felt himself free from all worries and problems.

All of a sudden, he heard a strange noise. It sounded like a moan or a wail. Hans followed the sound and discovered an injured bird on the ground. He picked it up and looked at it more closely. The bird was beautiful and Hans knew he had to help it.

He decided to take the bird home and take care of it. He fed it, gave it water and checked on its injuries. The bird recovered quickly and soon it was ready to be released back into the wild.

Hans brought the bird back to the mountains and let it fly. He watched it climb higher and higher and finally disappear in the sky. Hans felt an incredible joy and satisfaction. He knew that he had done something good and that he had given something back to nature.

At that moment, Hans realized that he would never stop loving and appreciating nature. The joy he felt while hiking and observing animals was indescribable. He knew that he would have many more adventures in nature and that they would always give him happiness and joy.

The day at the amusement park

Kurt was 70 years old, but he still had a young man's sense of adventure. He had always enjoyed fast roller coasters and white water rides, but it had been a while since he had last visited an amusement park.

One day he decided to treat himself to a day at the amusement park. He wasn't sure if he had the same energy as before, but he was willing to give it a try. He bought his ticket, got a pass and set off.

He was overwhelmed by all the different attractions to experience. The roller coasters were higher, faster and steeper than he could remember. But he wasn't deterred, he tried them all. It was like a rush and he couldn't get enough of it.

When he took a short break, he met a group of seniors who were also enjoying themselves at the amusement park. They were sitting on a bench and drinking coffee. Kurt joined them and they began to talk. It turned out that they were all friends from the neighborhood and that they went to the amusement park together every year.

They invited Kurt to come with them and he agreed. Together they visited the various attractions and had a lot of fun. Kurt felt like a young man and enjoyed the company of the other seniors.

When the day ended, Kurt was full of energy and happiness. He was grateful that he had embarked on the adventure at the amusement park and that he had made new friends. He realized that it's never too late to have fun and that life can be full of surprises and joy.

The trip abroad

Maria had always been an adventurer and had taken many trips in her life. But there was one thing she had never done: travel abroad. She had always dreamed of visiting other countries and learning about new cultures.

When she turned 75, she decided to make her dream come true. She booked a trip to Spain, a country she had always been fascinated by. She was a little apprehensive because she would be traveling alone and also because she didn't speak the Spanish language well. But she was not deterred and set off.

Arriving in Spain, Maria was fascinated by the beauty of the country and the friendliness of the people. She immediately felt at home and enjoyed every moment of her trip. She visited the sights, sampled the local food and drinks, and spent a lot of time strolling through the picturesque streets of the cities.

One day she met a group of seniors who were also traveling alone. They got to talking and soon they had decided to continue their journey together. They visited other cities together and had a lot of fun together.

Maria was grateful for these new friends and for the opportunity to share her journey. She realized that it is never too late to have new adventures and make new friends. At the end of her journey, she was happier and more fulfilled than ever before.

When Maria returned home, she had many stories to tell and new friends to keep in touch with. She was grateful for this wonderful journey and that she had finally realized her dream.

The visit to the hairdresser

Gertrud had been wearing the same haircut and hairstyle for years and felt somewhat dissatisfied with her appearance. One day she decided to try something new and venture a visit to the hairdresser.

She looked for a hair salon nearby and made an appointment. On the day of her appointment, Gertrud was a little excited, but also full of anticipation. She knew that a new hairstyle would boost her confidence.

When she entered the salon, she was greeted by a friendly staff who offered her a coffee and sat her in a comfortable hairdressing chair. Gertrud told the hairdresser that she was ready for a change and they chatted about various options.

Finally, Gertrud decided on a chic short hairstyle that would highlight her face. The hairdresser started cutting and Gertrud could hardly wait to see the result.

When he finished, Gertrud turned to the mirror and could hardly believe it. She looked so much younger and more alive and her eyes were shining with joy. The hairdresser had implemented her wishes perfectly.

Gertrud thanked the hairdresser and left the salon with a new bounce in her step. She felt happy and renewed and couldn't wait to show all her friends her new hairstyle.

In the days that followed, Gertrud received many compliments on her new hairstyle and she felt uplifted. She knew she had done the right thing by choosing a new look.

From that day on, going to the hairdresser became a regular part of Gertrud's beauty routine and she enjoyed the change and the feeling of pampering herself every time.

The discovery of the new

Hans had been a pensioner for many years and had already gained a lot of experience in his life. He had traveled a lot in the past, tried many hobbies and made many friends. But lately he had the feeling that something was missing, as if life no longer offered him any challenges.

One day, while looking for a book at the library, he came across a group of people talking about a new hobby - geocaching. Hans had never heard of it, and when he inquired, the people explained to him that it involves finding and collecting hidden items outdoors by following coordinated clues on a GPS app.

Hans was fascinated by the idea and decided to give it a try. He downloaded the GPS app and started looking for the first clues. It wasn't easy, but Hans quickly found that he enjoyed being outdoors, discovering new places, and solving puzzles along the way.

Over time, Hans got better at geocaching and he found out that there was a whole community of people who met regularly to go treasure hunting together. He joined them and quickly made new friends who shared the joy of discovering the new just like he did.

Geocaching not only brought Hans new friends, but also a new perspective on life. He discovered that there is still so much to learn and experience, and that it's never too late to try something new.

When Hans went home at the end of the day, he was full of joy and gratitude for discovering geocaching. He knew that he had found something that gave him new energy and enthusiasm, and that he could still discover new things in his old age.

The encounter with animals

Katharina has always been an animal lover. When she became a pensioner, she finally had more time to devote to her passion. One day she decided to take a trip to the nearby animal park. She had often heard about this park, but had never been there.

When she entered the park, she was immediately excited. All around her were beautiful animals, from large lions and elephants to small monkeys and parrots. Catherine could hardly hide her joy and enthusiastically wandered through the park to see every animal.

While wandering through the park, she noticed a small stand where an animal keeper was presenting some animals. Catherine was fascinated and watched intently as the keeper took a small rabbit out of its crate. The rabbit looked so cute that she wanted to pet it, and when the keeper offered it to her, she didn't hesitate.

When she held the rabbit in her hands, she felt it was soft and warm. She could feel the joy that the little animal gave her, and she couldn't help but smile. The caregiver told her that the rabbit was a special kind of therapy animal and that it helped other people relax and recover.

Katharina was impressed and decided to learn more about therapy animals. She started doing research and discovered that there was an animal therapy facility near her. She decided to go there and get involved, so she started spending time with animals on a regular basis.

Catherine found that meeting animals gave her a new joy and a new meaning in her life. She helped care for the animals and learned how to communicate with them and how to give them love and attention. She felt fulfilled and happy, and she knew she would enjoy her passion for animals for many years to come.

The trip to the mountains

Anna was an energetic retiree and still had a passion for adventure and travel. She had visited many places around the world, but there was one place she had always wanted to visit: the mountains. She had always imagined what it would be like to stand on a peak and enjoy the majestic view.

One day she decided it was time to make her dream come true. She planned a trip to the mountains and organized everything from start to finish. She booked a cabin in the mountains and invited some of her friends to join her.

When they arrived in the mountains, the view was breathtaking. The clear air and spectacular scenery took their breath away. The group hiked through the mountains, enjoying the fresh air and beautiful surroundings.

One day they decided to hike to the highest peak. It was a challenge, but they were all full of energy and looking forward to the view from the top. They hiked all day and finally reached the top just as the sun began to set.

The view from the top was spectacular. They could see the surrounding mountains and valleys, and the sunset turned the sky a warm orange and red. Anna and her friends felt incredibly happy and fulfilled. It was an unforgettable moment and an experience they would cherish for a lifetime.

When they returned to their hut in the evening, they were tired but happy. They sat around the fire and shared their experiences and impressions of the day. It was a moment full of joy and fellowship, and Anna felt grateful for the experience she had had.

The trip to the mountains had brought Anna and her friends not only breathtaking scenery and wonderful memories, but also the joy of life and nature. They knew they had many adventures and trips ahead of them in the future, but this moment in the mountains would always be special.

The visit to the optician

In the small town where Emma lives, there is only one optician. One day, when Emma noticed that her eyes were a bit strained when reading and watching TV, she decided to make an appointment with him.

She was a little nervous, not knowing what to expect. She had never worn glasses before, and although she knew it helped a lot of people, she was afraid it would make her look older.

When Emma entered the optician, she was greeted by a friendly voice. The optician, Mr. Schmidt, was an older man with a calm demeanor. He asked Emma some questions about her visual habits and examined her eyes.

Emma was amazed at how quick and easy the examination was. When Mr. Schmidt showed her some frames that might suit her, she could hardly decide. She tried on one after the other and each time Mr. Schmidt said how good she looked.

After some time, Emma had decided on a pair of glasses. Mr. Schmidt put in the lenses and adjusted the temples so that they fit perfectly. Emma was amazed at how clear and sharp she could suddenly see.

She had not expected the visit to the optician to be so pleasant. Mr. Schmidt was so nice and helpful and had helped her find glasses that not only helped her see better, but also looked good.

When Emma went outside, she could see the world around her much better. She saw the details in the leaves of the trees and the colors of the flowers much more clearly than before. It was as if a new world opened up for her.

Emma was so grateful for Mr. Schmidt's experience and help. She not only felt better, but younger and more vital. The visit to the optometrist was a real pleasure for her and she would recommend it to anyone who has problems with their eyes.

The joy of movement

Mrs. Müller had always been a passionate dancer. But with age, her joints had become stiffer and she had had to retire from her beloved hobby. One day, however, while out for a walk, she heard music coming from a nearby park. Curious, she followed the sound and found a group of people moving to happy music.

It was a group of seniors who were doing sports together and having a lot of fun. Ms. Müller joined them and was immediately warmly welcomed. The group did various exercises to loosen joints and strengthen muscles. Then the music started and the group danced together.

Mrs. Müller felt her joints becoming more mobile again and her mood getting better and better. The other seniors were full of joy and laughed and sang to the music. Mrs. Müller felt like she was in her youth and danced along enthusiastically.

Since that day, she regularly participated in the group's activities. She met new friends and had found joy in exercise again. Her body became fitter again and her mood also improved. She was happy and grateful for this wonderful experience and knew that it was never too late to enjoy exercise.

The encounter with other cultures

Mrs. Schmidt had always been a curious woman and had always dreamed of getting to know other cultures. But due to her responsibilities as a single mother and later as a working woman, she had never had the opportunity to travel.

But when she retired, she decided to finally make that dream come true. She signed up for a group trip and traveled to a faraway country. At first, she felt a bit unsure and foreign in the new environment. But she was quickly surprised by the hospitality of the locals.

She began to discover the new culture and learned how people lived there. She tried new food and learned new words in a different language. Ms. Schmidt was amazed by the beauty of the country and the friendliness of the people.

In one of the next day's tours, she met a group of elderly locals who invited her to their home. They were warmly welcomed by the family and spent the day sharing stories and eating together. Ms. Schmidt realized that despite the differences in culture and language, they all had similar values and desires.

The trip was an unforgettable experience for Ms. Schmidt and she returned home filled with joy and gratitude for the opportunity to learn about other cultures. She had made new friends and seen the world through new eyes. It was clear to her that it is never too late to discover something new and that it is always possible to build bridges between cultures.

The visit to the Christmas market

It was just before Christmas and Anna couldn't wait to visit the Christmas market. She loved the smell of roasted almonds and mulled wine, the lights and the festive atmosphere. Together with her friend Lisa, whom she had known for years, she had planned this day for a long time.

When they entered the Christmas market, they were greeted by a sea of lights and colors. Colorful Christmas decorations hung everywhere and it smelled like cinnamon and cloves. Anna could feel her mood brightening, and she enjoyed every moment.

She and Lisa strolled through the alleys and admired the many stalls selling artistic handicrafts, delicious delicacies and Christmas decorations. They sampled mulled wine and hot chocolate, ate roasted almonds and gingerbread hearts, and enjoyed the pre-Christmas atmosphere.

Suddenly Anna stopped at a stand where homemade candles were offered. She looked at the beautiful colors and patterns and decided to buy a few as Christmas gifts. While talking to the vendor, she noticed that he had a foreign accent and asked him where he was from. He told her about his home in the south and the Christmas traditions there. Anna listened enthusiastically to his stories and felt herself discovering a new culture.

In the late afternoon, as the sun slowly set and the Christmas market gradually emptied, Anna and Lisa sat in a café drinking tea. They talked about the day and how nice it was to enjoy the festive atmosphere together. Anna talked about her conversation with the candle seller and how much she had enjoyed discovering something new.

When they finally got up to go home, Anna felt a warm feeling of joy and happiness in her heart. She knew that this day was one of her best Christmas market visits and that she was looking forward to more adventures and discoveries in her life.

The challenges of old age

The sun was shining in the sky as Emma looked out the window, wondering what the day would bring. She had been retired for several years and was enjoying her life to the fullest. But lately she felt that her life had become a little monotonous.

That day, Emma decided to do something adventurous. She knew that at 75 years old she was no longer the youngest, but that didn't stop her from taking on new challenges.

She decided to go for a hike in the mountains. After changing her clothes and packing her gear, she set off. The mountains were not too far from her house and she had often thought about exploring them.

The hike was more strenuous than Emma had expected, but she enjoyed every moment of it. The view of the mountains and the fresh air did her good, and she felt more alive than ever. Along the way, she met other hikers who were all very friendly and helpful.

After a few hours, Emma reached the top. The view from up there was breathtaking, and she felt happy and satisfied. It was a moment she would never forget.

On the way back, she met a couple her age who had also hiked. They got to talking and realized they had many interests in common. They decided to stay in touch and meet again.

When Emma came home that evening, she felt exhausted but also fulfilled. She had mastered a new challenge and made new friends. It made her feel that life still had many adventures in store for her, and she was ready to take them on.

The joy of craftsmanship

Emma has always been an avid crafter. She always enjoyed creating and designing things with her own hands. Whether it was clothing, decorations or furniture, Emma always had new ideas and projects in mind.

But since she retired and her children were out of the house, Emma felt that her passion for crafts was slowly fading. She felt she was losing her skills and moving away from her creative spirit.

One day, while Emma was walking through the park, she met a group of people who were organizing an exhibition of handmade items. Emma was fascinated by the various booths, which ranged from handmade clothing and jewelry to wood carvings and pottery.

As she looked around, Emma noticed an elderly woman sitting at a stall selling handmade baskets. Emma was fascinated by the beauty and simplicity of the baskets and began talking to the woman. The two chatted about her passion for the craft and Emma told the woman about her own experiences and projects.

The woman smiled at Emma and asked her if she had ever thought of making her own handmade baskets. Emma was hesitant at first, but the woman encouraged her to give it a try and rediscover her skills.

Emma bought a small instruction book and started to make her first baskets. It was difficult at first and she had to practice a lot, but eventually she developed her own technique and was able to design and make her own baskets.

The joy and happiness Emma felt while crafting returned and she felt her passion for crafting reignited. Emma began selling her baskets at the weekly market and soon became a well-known craftswoman in town.

For Emma, it was not only a joy to express her creativity and talent, but also a way to meet new people and share her passion for the craft with others.

The visit to the dentist

It was a sunny day in spring and Maria had an appointment with the dentist. She had been a customer of his for many years and always felt comfortable in his practice. But this time something was different. Maria had not been feeling quite well for the last few weeks and was afraid that her dentist might discover something bad.

When she entered the practice, she was greeted by the friendly receptionist and took a seat in the waiting room. There she met an elderly lady named Helga, whom she had never seen before. Helga was a bit nervous and started talking to Maria to distract herself. The two women exchanged stories about their hobbies, their families, and their experiences at the dentist.

After some time, Maria was called and entered the treatment room. Her dentist, Dr. Müller, greeted her in a friendly manner and began the examination. Maria felt that she was very tense, but Dr. Müller calmed her down and explained every step of the process.

Meanwhile, they suddenly heard a loud bang from the next room. Dr. Müller apologized to Maria and left the room to see what had happened. When he returned, he explained that one of the chairs in the next room was broken and that she would therefore have to wait a little longer for her treatment.

Maria had some time to think and relax. When Dr. Müller finally returned, she was surprised that he asked her if she would bring Helga, the elderly lady from the waiting room, into the treatment room with her. After all, Helga didn't have a car and couldn't make her way to another dentist.

Maria agreed and Dr. Müller took Helga out of the waiting room. The two women exchanged pleasantries and Maria noticed that Helga was really excited, but also very happy to be with her.

Dr. Müller began treating Maria and Helga sat next to her and held her hand. Maria felt so reassured and taken care of that she almost forgot she was at the dentist.

When the treatment was over and Maria and Helga left the practice, both women felt happy and relieved. They had helped each other and made a new friendship. Maria knew she was still concerned about her health, but she also felt empowered and safe to share such an experience.

This day at the dentist had not only fixed Maria and Helga's teeth, but also opened their hearts and created new friendships.

The encounter with technology

Sophie has always been curious and open to new things. But when she received a laptop as a gift from her grandson, she was skeptical. Technology and computers were something completely new and unknown to her. But Sophie was ready to take on the challenge and figure out how to make the most of her new gift.

She started by searching for tutorials on YouTube and signing up for computer classes in her area. It wasn't long before she felt more comfortable with technology and began exploring her digital world.

With her new knowledge and skills, Sophie began impressing her friends and family with her abilities. She sent them emails and messages, made video calls and shared her experiences on social media. The joy she felt was indescribable.

Sophie had been transformed by her encounter with technology. She had left her comfort zone and acquired new skills that enriched her life. It was a challenge, but it was also a source of joy and happiness.

The joy of cooking

Inge was a spry retiree who had lived alone in her house since her husband died five years ago. She had always enjoyed cooking, but since she was alone, she had found it difficult to find motivation to cook. Her children and grandchildren visited her regularly and often brought her ready-made meals, but Inge didn't want to live on ready-made food alone. She longed for the joy and creativity that cooking had brought her in the past.

One day, Inge saw an ad for a cooking class for seniors at the local community hall. Although nervous, she signed up, looking forward to the chance to learn new cooking techniques and make new friends.

On the day of the course, she met a group of seniors who were as enthusiastic about cooking as she was. The teacher was an experienced chef and taught them how to enhance classic dishes with modern techniques and ingredients. Inge was especially excited about the tips on preparing vegetables and making her own spice blends.

She worked hard in class and took pride in the dishes she prepared. After each class, she would bring her creations home and share them with her neighbors and friends. She also invited her family over for a big meal where she could proudly demonstrate the new skills she had learned.

Inge learned not only how to cook better, but also how to make new friends and live out her passions as she got older. She was thrilled with the joy that cooking brought back to her and knew that she was now able to create delicious meals for herself whenever she wanted.

The visit to the theater

Hanna and her friends had been looking forward to this day for weeks - a visit to the theater was on the agenda! It had been a long time since they had had such an opportunity, and they were excited at the prospect of immersing themselves in the world of culture.

It was a sunny day when they met and drove to the theater together. The streets were full of people enjoying the beautiful weather, but the women had only the theater on their minds. They talked about their expectations and anticipation of the play they would see.

When they reached the theater, they were impressed by the elegant facade and majestic architecture. Inside, they were overwhelmed by the ambiance and elegant décor of the theater. There was soft lighting that filled the room with warmth and atmosphere, and their anticipation for the play increased.

They took their seats and enjoyed waiting for the play to begin. When the performance finally began, the mood became quiet and expectant. The stage shone in the spotlight and the play began.

It was an emotional and moving performance about life and love, and the women were deeply touched by the message of the play. They laughed, cried and applauded enthusiastically at the end of the performance.

When they left the theater, they were full of enthusiasm and gratitude for the experience they had. They felt invigorated and inspired by the art and culture they had experienced. It was an unforgettable day, and they knew they would carry those memories in their hearts forever.

The discovery of life

Catherine had just turned 70 and decided it was time to try something new. She had worked hard all her life and raised her children, but now she felt the need to do more with her life. One day, she learned about a group of seniors who met regularly to share new experiences and enjoy life together. Katharina was immediately enthusiastic and decided to join them.

The group met once a week and undertook various activities. Sometimes they went hiking together, sometimes they visited a museum or they took part in cooking classes. It was a colorful group of people, all of senior age, but still full of joie de vivre and curiosity.

Katharina quickly made friends in the group and looked forward to the next meeting every time. One day, one of the participants suggested that they go on a trip together. It should be a trip that would challenge them all and where they could gain new experiences together. After some discussion, they agreed to travel to India.

Katharina had never traveled outside of Europe before and was a little nervous at first. But her new friends encouraged her and promised her that it would be an unforgettable experience. And so they set off together.

The trip was an adventure. They visited temples and palaces, explored the exotic nature and tried many new foods. The people were friendly and hospitable, and Catherine felt herself gaining more confidence and courage every day. The trip was a discovery of life for her, a revelation that it is never too late to discover new things.

At the end of the trip, they all returned happy and full of new experiences. Katharina felt that she had discovered a whole new world, and she knew that she would never forget the adventure. Not only had she discovered life in India, but she had also found a new side to herself. And she was grateful for having had the opportunity to experience all of this, thanks to the joy of life and the discovery of the unknown.

The journey into history

It was a sunny day in spring when Mrs. Müller decided to visit the Museum of History. She had always had a great interest in past eras and was curious to see what she would discover in the museum.

As she walked through the entrance hall, she felt like a time traveler transported back to another era. All around her were artifacts and exhibits from different times. Ms. Müller walked through the different exhibition areas, looking at ancient coins, old weapons and tools and learning more about the history of her city.

During her tour, she also met other visitors who were also interested in the past. They began to talk and shared their knowledge with each other. Ms. Müller found these encounters very enriching and enjoyed making new friends.

When she finally made it to the exit, she felt fulfilled and satisfied. She had learned a lot and was impressed by the beauty and diversity of the exhibits. But most of all, she was grateful for the opportunity to immerse herself in history and learn about her city's past.

On the way back home, she thought about how important it is to know and appreciate the past. She decided to visit the museum more often and continue her journey of discovery into history. Because, as she had realized, there was still so much to learn and discover.

The visit to the zoo

It was a sunny day when Mr. Müller decided to visit the zoo. He had not made such an excursion for years and was very excited. He loved animals and still remembered his childhood when he often visited the zoo with his parents.

When he arrived at the zoo, he was impressed by the variety of animals he saw. He saw elephants, giraffes, lions and even penguins! He took his time to explore each animal area and spent some time observing and admiring the animals.

Then he noticed a group of seniors who were together and seemed to be having a lot of fun. They were also at the zoo enjoying the animals like Mr. Miller. He decided to join them and ask if he could hang out with them.

The group welcomed him warmly and started showing him the different animals they had already seen. Mr. Müller thought it was great to get in touch with other people and exchange ideas.

They wandered around the zoo enjoying the animals, laughing and sharing memories of their previous visits to the zoo. It was a wonderful day, full of joy and happiness.

When the group parted to go their separate ways, Mr. Müller felt satisfied and fulfilled. He was grateful for the day and the encounter with the other seniors, which had given him such a positive experience.

On the way home, he thought about how important it was to stay in touch with other people and share joy and happiness together. The visit to the zoo was an unforgettable experience for him, which showed him that life can bring joy at any age.

The joy of reading

Anna has always been a passionate reader. Even as a child, she could sink into books for hours and was fascinated every time by the stories and adventures that took place in them. But in the course of her life she had found less and less time for reading. There was always something more important to do or take care of, and so reading had become less and less important.

But when Anna retired, that all changed. She finally had time again to devote to her favorite hobby. She regularly visited the local library and spent hours browsing through the shelves and picking out new books. She had started to lose herself in the stories again and couldn't get enough of them.

One day, while visiting the library, Anna met another reader who was also retired. The two exchanged stories about their favorite books and eventually decided to start their own reading group. They invited a few other seniors who also loved to read, and so a small community of like-minded people was born.

Every month, they met in a cozy café to discuss the current book. It was a highlight for Anna and the others to share ideas and learn new perspectives in the group. They often came back from their meetings inspired to read more and lose themselves in new stories.

Anna was happy to have time for her passion again and to exchange ideas with other readers. Reading had enriched her life and inspired her to remain curious and open to new things even in old age.

The encounter with literature

Mr. Fischer sat comfortably in his armchair and flipped through the pages of his favorite book. He had always loved to read and this had not changed even in his old age. That afternoon, he was particularly looking forward to reading, because he had received an invitation to a reading in the library.

The librarian had published an announcement in the local newspaper and Mr. Fischer had immediately decided to attend.

He had not attended such an event for a long time and was eager to meet other literature enthusiasts.

When he arrived at the library, he saw many other seniors who had also come to witness the reading. Mr. Fischer quickly found a seat and waited anxiously for the event to begin.

The author finally took the podium and presented her book. She read selected passages and told about the background of her work. Mr. Fischer was immediately captivated by the story and hung on her lips.

After the reading, there was a discussion session where the visitors could ask their questions to the author. Mr. Fischer also had a question and the author answered it in detail. He was enthusiastic about her enthusiasm for literature and the passion with which she had written her book.

When the reading was over, Mr. Fischer left the library with a broad smile on his face. He felt inspired and fulfilled by the encounter with literature. It had been a wonderful afternoon and he knew that he would now enjoy reading even more.

The day in the swimming pool

Gretel had not been to the swimming pool for years. She had forgotten how much pleasure swimming gave her. One day, however, she decided to embark on the adventure again.

The sun was shining and Gretel took the bus to the swimming pool. She hesitated briefly before entering the changing room. But when she dove into the pool, she felt like a child jumping into the pool. The coolness of the water and the movement her body made filled her with joy.

Gretel did her laps and chatted with other swimmers. Time flew by and she was disappointed when it was time to get out of the water. But as she gathered her things and got dressed, she noticed that her body felt invigorated and energized.

During the ride back home, Gretel could not stop thinking about the wonderful experience. She knew that she would go to the pool regularly to maintain the feeling of joy and vitality that swimming had brought her.

The challenge of hiking

Elisabeth is 67 years old and has lived in the city all her life. She loved to go for walks and explore the surroundings, but she had never had the chance to go hiking. Until one day she decided she wanted a new challenge. Elisabeth heard about a local hiking group and decided to join them.

On the day of the hike, Elisabeth was very excited. She met the group and learned that she would be hiking with other elderly people. The group was very friendly and supportive, and Elisabeth felt right at home. The hike took her through a picturesque landscape and Elisabeth enjoyed the fresh air and the tranquility of nature.

But soon the hike became more difficult than she had expected. The path led steeply uphill and Elisabeth began to sweat and gasp. She was about to give up when one of the group members offered her a helping hand and encouraged her to keep going.

Elisabeth suddenly felt her legs getting stronger and her heartbeat calmer. She was so proud of herself when she reached the top and saw the breathtaking view. The group cheered her and hugged her when she arrived.

At the end of the day, Elisabeth was happy and satisfied. She had faced a challenge and mastered it. She had made new friends and explored a beautiful landscape. She knew she would hike more often in the future and looked forward to the next adventures with her new hiking group.

The visit to the hearing care professional

Ingeborg could no longer hear the birds in her garden. The telephone also often rang unnoticed. Her husband had noticed it long ago and encouraged her to have a hearing test. "It will change you," he had said.

Ingeborg was skeptical, but she was afraid of missing out on more. So she made an appointment with a hearing aid acoustician. The young man greeted her warmly and led her into a small room where he examined her ears. "You have a hearing loss," he said. "But don't worry, we can help you."

He explained the different types of hearing aids and helped her choose the right model. Ingeborg was impressed by the modern technology and was amazed at how small and unobtrusive the hearing aids were. The acoustician also showed her how to clean and care for the devices.

When Ingeborg put in her new hearing aids, she was initially surprised by the many sounds she could hear again. But then she was overwhelmed by a wave of joy when she could hear the birds in her garden again. She could also now clearly hear her granddaughter calling her.

Ingeborg's husband was overjoyed when he saw how happy she was. He took her for a walk in the park and they enjoyed the sounds of nature together. Ingeborg was grateful that she had gotten up the nerve to visit the hearing care professional. She had not expected it to change her life so much, but she was happy that she could hear everything again.

The experiences in retirement

Anna had worked hard all her life and was looking forward to her well-deserved retirement. Finally, she could spend her time doing all the things she had always wanted to do. She had a stack of books waiting to be read, and she was looking forward to trying out new recipes and maybe even learning a craft or two.

But retirement also brought unexpected adventures. One day, Anna had decided to take a long walk in the park. She loved nature and the feeling of being outside in the fresh air. As she set off, she circled the lake and wandered through the woods, but after a while she realized she was lost.

Panic rose in her as she wasn't sure where she was or how to get back. But fortunately, she soon met a friendly couple who escorted her back to the park exit.

The adventure had boosted Anna's confidence and motivated her to experience even more new things. She enrolled in a group of like-minded people who went on trips once a month to explore new places. It was a great way to make new friends and see new parts of the world at the same time.

But there were also times when Anna just wanted to relax and unwind. On those days, she would sit on her terrace with a good book and enjoy the sunlight and fresh air. She also found joy in visiting her grandchildren and playing with them.

Anna learned that retirement can be a time of freedom, discovery and joy. She knew there would be challenges and adventures, but she was ready to accept and embrace them. Each day brought new experiences and opportunities, and she looked forward to seeing what would come next.

Imprint

LIOM LIOM
AUF DER HÖH 13A
35447 REISKIRCHEN
CONTACT
E-MAIL: sl350sl@gmx.de

Don't miss out!

Visit the website below and you can sign up to receive emails whenever Liom Liom publishes a new book. There's no charge and no obligation.

https://books2read.com/r/B-A-AOUW-GMRGC

BOOKS2READ

Connecting independent readers to independent writers.

Did you love *Stories for Seniors*? Then you should read *Stories That Make you Happy*[1] by Liom Liom!

Experience the beauty of life now in this unique paperback and be enchanted by stories that touch the heart and make you happy. These inspiring short stories explore themes such as the power of thought, the joy of discovery, or the path to fulfillment - each one telling in its own way about the beauty in the here and now and the happiness that surrounds us. Let yourself be enchanted by these stories and find new perspectives that will enrich your life.

---

1. https://books2read.com/u/bxry2J

2. https://books2read.com/u/bxry2J